Lesson for the Wolf

Published by Inhabit Media Inc. • www.inhabitmedia.com

Inhabit Media Inc. (Iqaluit), P.O. Box 11125, Iqaluit, Nunavut, XOA 1HO
(Toronto), 146A Orchard View Blvd., Toronto, Ontario, M4R 1C3

Editors: Neil Christopher and Louise Flaherty
Art director: Danny Christopher

We acknowledge the financial support of the Government of Canada through the Department of Canadian Heritage Canada Book Fund.

We acknowledge the support of the Canada Council for the Arts for our publishing program.

Printed in Canada

Canadian Heritage   Patrimoine canadien   Canadä   Canada Council for the Arts   Conseil des Arts du Canada

Library and Archives Canada Cataloguing in Publication

Qitsualik-Tinsley, Rachel, 1953-, author
     Lesson for the wolf / by Rachel and Sean Qitsualik-Tinsley ; illustrated
by Alan Cook.

ISBN 978-1-77227-005-1 (bound)

     I. Qitsualik-Tinsley, Sean, 1969- author II. Cook, Alan, illustrator
III. Title.

PS8633.I88L48 2015   jC813'.6   C2015-901354-2

Lesson for the Wolf

by Rachel and Sean Qitsualik-Tinsley

illustrated by Alan Cook

Have you seen the Land?

It was the Arctic: white in winter, brown in summer. There were mountains. Shining waters. No trees. But flowers lay like purple fire on the hills.

Have you felt the Strength of the Land?

Its Strength was its life. And that life was tied to every other life that flew, swam, or ran.

Have you heard of the wolf?

The one who disliked all the things that wolves enjoy?

Wolves dream of running free. But this wolf did not want to run.

　　Wolves love to play. Yet this wolf had no interest in the sports of his brothers and sisters.

　　Without him, the pack ran and played under a grand Sky (and if you've played under that same Sky, you know what a joy it is).

This wolf had one hobby: he liked to study other animals.

He crept up on caribou, but did not chase them. He sat and envied their tall, curving antlers.

He watched wolverines and admired their fine, bushy tails.

He found an owl's nest and spied on the mother, who sat on her eggs.
Her white feathers were lovely.

In time, the wolf no longer spoke to his brothers and sisters.
They grew annoyed with him. He participated very little in hunts.

One day, the wolf stood alone on a hilltop. His heart felt like it was breaking. He was filled with love of the Land. Of its beauty. He wanted to become part of it . . .

But how?

Just a wolf, he thought to himself. *I'm just a wolf.*

He turned his head to the Sky. The wolf sang of his unhappiness. He sang to the Land and its Strength.

He got wild ideas.

The wolf went and collected some fallen caribou antlers. These were easy to find. There were many caribou, and they shed their antlers every year. The wolf decided that, if caribou didn't want such lovely antlers, he could find a use for them.

He grabbed the best pair in sight.

Then the wolf scrounged up a bit of wolverine hair. This was unpleasant. Wolverines had the nicest coat of any animal. But they smelled bad. The wolf managed to find a place where a wolverine had eaten. Luckily, the wolverine had dropped a bit of hair.

The stink made the wolf dizzy.

Finally, the wolf worked up the courage to steal an owl feather. This didn't go well. Owls put their nests out on the open Land. The wolf thought that he might find a feather in such a nest. But when he came near, the father owl swooped at him with sharp talons.

Luckily, the angry bird dropped a feather. The wolf snatched it up and ran without looking back.

The wolf gathered his new treasures. Again, he sang to the Land. With all his broken heart, he sang.

And his own life moved with the life of the Land.

The Land's Strength gave him power. With that power in him, he pushed his head against the stubs of antler. There was a blur as they became part of him. He raised his tall, antlered head with pride.

The wolf placed the wolverine hairs near his tail. Instantly, his tail became orange and black. Bushy. Beautiful. It was the tail of a wolverine.

Lastly, the wolf rolled himself on the stolen owl feather. In a couple of heartbeats, the fur of his body began to change. Soon, it was smooth, purest white mottled with black. He was covered in snowy owl feathers.

The wolf yipped in delight. Happy at last, he played under the grand Sky. He was now perfect, a mixture of all the animals he had so admired.

A month later, the wolf crept back to his pack.
At first, his brothers and sisters laughed at his crazy
appearance. But they soon felt sorry for him.
He had no wings, so he could not hunt like an owl.
His nose was not as good as a wolverine's, so he could
not sniff out food for himself.
Their hearts broke as they watched him
nibble on lichen, like a caribou. He
always spat it out.

The pack tried to leave a bit of food for him. But he always ran from them, crying, "I'm not a wolf anymore!"

Secretly, he was embarrassed that he could not survive on his own. If he returned, ate their food, what would they think of him? He thought that they might laugh some more. He could not bear evil laughter—especially from those he loved.

He was starving.

Alone on a hill, under the grand Sky, he lay down. He was too sad to play. Too weak. Too lonely.

In time, the mother of the wolves came to him. She sat listening to the wind with him. And after a while, she asked, "Why are you so sad, my love? So weak? So lonely?"

"Oh, Mother," he wept, "I only wanted to be beautiful. But I was just a wolf . . ."

So his mother told him, "We wolves cry to the Moon, my love, because we admire its beauty. But you cannot admire beauty by becoming it. Then you will miss the greatest beauty that a wolf can know."

The wolf told her that he did not understand.

"It is better shown than told," said the mother of the wolves.

Then she called over the wolf's brothers. His sisters. She called even old ones and pups.

No one laughed as they gathered around him. Instead, they sang. In the way wolves do, they sang to the Land. And its Strength was moved by their love for him. And the Land undid all the changes it had made.

The wolf healed. In time, he hunted with his pack. He even played with them under the grand Sky.

More than ever before, the wolf admired beauty in other animals. Even those he hunted for food. Yet he never again wished for change. He came to see beauty in a wolf's life. For he now saw himself through the eyes of the pack.

He was a wolf—and that in itself was admirable.

Contributors

Born in an Arctic wilderness camp and of Inuit ancestry, **Rachel Qitsualik-Tinsley** is a scholar specializing in world religions and cultures. Her numerous articles and books concerning Inuit magic and lore have earned her a Queen Elizabeth II Diamond Jubilee Medal.

Of Scottish-Mohawk ancestry, **Sean Qitsualik-Tinsley** is a folklorist and fantasist, specializing in mythology, magic, and Inuit lore. He has won an award for writing short science fiction ("Green Angel"), but his focus is on fiction and non-fiction for a young audience.

Alan Cook is a kid from London, Ontario, who (arguably) grew up to be an artist. People mostly ask him to draw for animation, but above all he loves to tell stories using a pen and a paintbrush. He spends whatever time he can in the rugged outdoors of the Pacific Northwest or the sunny hills of Southern California. He hopes one day to grow up to have a real, respectable job, but will continue to paint and draw as long as people ask him to.

IQALUIT · TORONTO